Welcome to Wonderland

By Emma Russell

All rights reserved. No part of this publication may be reproduced, stored or transmitted in any form or by any means, electronic, mechanical, photocopying, recording, scanning, or otherwise without written permission from the publisher. It is illegal to copy this book, post it to a website, or distribute it by any other means without permission.

ISBN 978-1-7384046-0-5

This novel is entirely a work of fiction. The names, characters and incidents portrayed in it are the work of the author's imagination. Any resemblance to actual persons, living or dead, events or localities is entirely coincidental.

Cover Art by Emma Russell and Dorian Valentine
Illustrations by Emma Russell

Content Warning:

This book contains discussions around mental health, trauma and hospitalisation.

There are also scenes involving gaslighting and a scene which is an allusion to a suicide attempt.

While I drew from my own experiences, this book's narrative is fictional.

Dear Reader,

I've tried to write this opening note throughout the course of writing this book, and frankly I keep coming up empty on what exactly to say.

I've suffered with depression and anxiety for years, but it has finally reached a point in the past year where I couldn't take it any more. That's when I started writing this.

I wasn't able to communicate my feelings directly without being extremely self-critical, so the best way was to start hiding everything in metaphors and strange descriptions.

Originally, this was going to tell the story of Alice, my role-playing character with a dark past and who had to change her name. Then it became the story of Alice, the manifestation of my toxic feelings and thoughts.

Let me reassure you, I'm doing better. Some nights are harder than others, but I'm making sure I hold on.

I sincerely hope you enjoy this story.

Love, Emma

(Written in 2020)

Dear Reader,

Oh my goodness, I was right throwing myself a pity party in that first letter.

I'm a miserable one it seems.

It's been a while since I've touched this book, and properly looked through it. And here we are, three years later.

I'm still miserable, but not as much as before. So much of my life has changed for the better, and every day I learn a little more about myself. I'm grateful for the pain, even though it hurt, for I would not be the person I am without it.

Turns out, I wrote another note in 2019, right after the first draft was finished. I wrote about how a little bit of me was in Alice. Turns out, a *lot* of me was in Alice, more than I realised.

Therapy is important.

Anyway, the point is, I'm glad I'm still here. And I'm glad you are too.

You get to read the nice updated version, with its own ISBN and me finally deciding to stop being a coward and give the spelling and grammar a proper check over.

I'm so different now. It feels strange, reading through this story. Seeing every poisonous feeling and thought I had appear again.

If this new edition shows anything, is that things truly can get better.

Not perfect, and not fixed, but better.

I can feel content.

Alice is still a little bit of me. She is my desire to heal and do a little better each day.

This Alice will always be a part of me.

I like to give my characters somewhat happy endings. Realistic happy endings. Even beyond what I've written.

So here's one for you.

Alice never went back to the room of white. Peter is still always at her side, and the only wonderland she experiences is the one in the books.

She is well. And one day, you will be too. Alice and I believe in you.

With hope and love, Em

(Written in 2023)

This book, or story, or whatever name we wish to call it, is dedicated to the wonderfully glorious Dorian.

For without them, Alice would not have a reason to be created, and I would not be compelled to tell her story.

A Call to Arms

I think it's time

                        Oh, is it now?

                It's time for us to do something

Is it necessary?

Oh, very necessary, I barely recognise her

    He's to blame

    What a shame

                          That it had to come to this

                I know.

What if she's too far gone   It'll only work if we do it together

We know what we are to her

We're not real

But we have a responsibility

                                                          Fine.

                                                         Fine.

            What should we do?

Whatever we must do to make her

Change her mind

                                  change her mind

                         Change her mind

change her mind

Down You Go, All Alone

Alice was in the room of white. She was sitting on a white bed, with its white sheet and white pillow. Her black shoes rested on the white tiled floor. Her knees were trembling. She interlaced the thin pale fingers on her thin pale hands and rested them in her lap. Her black skirt tickled her thin pale skin. She both liked and disliked the sensation.

As her eyes peered forward, along with her head, her shoulders, and torso, she looked down at the floor. She saw the white turn to black, and it started to cave in on itself. Her breathing stopped. The only sound up to that point had been her breathing, and now that she had silenced that noise, there was nothing left. Fear was hanging in the air like a rotten disease.

The floor continued to sink, and soon Alice's shoes began to sink with it, along with her feet and legs. She tried to scream, but there was no sound because there was no air. After all, she had stopped breathing, and because she had stopped breathing nobody would hear her screams.

So, she let herself sink. She didn't dare to breathe, or scream, for she knew none of that would matter in the grand scheme of things anyway since nothing like this ever happened.

She left the room of white. Her head was swallowed by the floor and suddenly she was falling. It wasn't fast, nor slow, it was a gradual descent, and Alice finally allowed herself to breathe again. She seemed to be falling down a tunnel. It was dark, but not dark, and light but not light. There was an array of colours, and they hurt her eyes, so she shut them. She welcomed the darkness, but despite it, the colours still flashed behind her eyelids.

She felt objects knock into her as she went down, which forced her to open her eyes once more to see what she was impacting with. She noticed common household objects rose around her. Everything from worn-out recipe books covered in flour to broken teacups and plates. There were some knives too, sharp horrible things which Alice curled away from so she wouldn't be hit by them. Ripped-out papers flew past at quickening speeds. Alice grabbed a couple and noticed they were pages from books she read. She recognised passages and remembered the words that had been poured out of them. Another gush of wind arrived, and brushed the papers out of her hand, sending them back up the tunnel.

Slightly let down by the turn of events, Alice shut her eyes again, waiting for the whole sequence to be over and done with.

After some time, she stopped falling through the tunnel, and she emerged out the other end. She was greeted by a bright blue sky, which had blends of green swirling through it like it was plucked straight out of the river. She fell to the ground. The ground was a cobblestone path in the middle of a field with slowly dying grass. She landed on the ground with a gentle crash. Alice wasn't hurt, but just slightly shaken.

She looked ahead of her and noticed the forest looming ahead. Even though it looked dark, it probably wasn't, as she recognised this place, even if it was slightly different. The forest itself was not too far from her, but its trees were tall, and their trunks spread wide, so she could not see what was beyond them. When she looked up, the tunnel she had fallen down was gone completely, and only the sky was left. When she turned around, she saw a great, long stone wall behind her, with no clear indication of how to get past it.

This supposedly was the beginning. Perhaps there would be an end as well.

Alice, with her shaking legs, stood up. She took a moment to compose herself, and to make herself look a fraction more presentable than she did at this point. She flattened her hands out along her skirt, smoothing out the creases, and raised her hands to her hair, pulling at her bow to tighten it.

She then handled the task of looking towards the forest. There was only one way in it seemed. A single path led into an arched entrance, where the trees bent their branches to clearly show that this was the way to go. However, before Alice could start making her way there, someone walked towards her.

At first, she could not see who it was. But, when they finally appeared into view, her dark eyes widened and sparkled with hope.

She looked at the person as he stopped in front of her. He was wearing bright blue striped trousers, and a matching jacket with three long tailcoats. The jacket was unbuttoned, with a white ruffled shirt beneath it, and a red ribbon tied in a bow at his collar. His skin was pale, and his eyes were a dazzling blue, and he had bright fiery curly red hair that was hidden beneath the most astounding hat she had ever seen.

It was a bright blue, like his eyes, with a jungle green ribbon wrapped around it. There were four playing cards tucked into this ribbon, along with a spoon.

Alice clapped her hands and let out a sob. "Hatter!" The figure looked as equally happy and surprised as she did. "Ello Ali!"

Hatter bounded forward and pulled her into a hug. She stiffened slightly at the touch, at the feeling of somebody being this close to her. But this was Hatter, and she knew Hatter better than she knew most people.

When he pulled away, Alice saw his bright smile. "It's been so long! We haven't talked in *forever* Ali! Where 'av you been?"

Alice felt her heart clench for a moment.

"I…I've been getting help Hatter, you know that. I'm sorry."

Hatter looked as if the world had suddenly stopped and that the sky was falling directly above them.

His eyes were staring, and his bright smile was twitching a little bit. "Oh well…it doe matter now does it? You're back, an' that's all that matters!"

She lifted her head and looked around. She looked at the sky, the forest, and the wall. "Wonderland has changed a lot since I was last here."

He pouted. "That's cause ya stopped visiting! I had to come to visit *you* which was 'ard cause of those stupid bloody mushrooms!"

As Hatter spoke, Alice noticed the volume and intensity of his voice rose with every word. He did that often like his own speech was out of his control somehow. Sometimes his voice, and almost all of the time his words, scared her. When he noticed that her eyes looked like a creature that had been caught in the lights at the front of those metal boxes, he paused. He straightened his bowtie and realigned his hat, which had somehow tilted itself.

"Anyhow, you're 'ere now, and that's all that matters. There ain't no need for you to go rushing back there."

Alice's head leaned to the side a little. "Perhaps you're right Hatter."

He grinned. "That's cause I'm always right!" He did a little jump with joy. "Come along then! Lemme show ya around!"

Hatter started walking towards the forest, and Alice carefully followed him. "Around to where?" She asked.

Hatter chuckled. It was an oddly deep rumbling sound. "I dunno actually, let's go find out."

He skipped as he walked, his steps springing off the ground and giving him a small amount of elevation. Alice walked briskly beside him, her footsteps methodical and in time with his springs.

The two of them, and their oddly differentiating steps, headed towards the branched archway that served as the entrance to the forest. As they approached it, Alice noticed how dark the branches and the trunks of the trees looked. They weren't brown per se, like one would expect trees to be. They had a darkish blue tint to them. Alice wondered if a pack of playing cards had been allowed near a tin of blue paint and a brush. The leaves were also dark, but they kept their green colour, although some parts had turned black.

Perhaps this meant they were dying, but Alice couldn't remember what season it was.

Hatter jumped through the archway and gestured for Alice to follow. When Alice stepped through, and her first step landed in the forest, she felt a chill ripple through her. She didn't like it. It reminded her of sharp metal, of the slices through her skin. Her thin pale hand reached for her cheek, to see if the chill had reached there.

"Come on Ali!" Hatter called, as he stopped and turned around on one foot.

Alice took a breath, as she had been taught by a man she couldn't remember. Now was not the time for this. This feeling would only cause trouble for both herself and everyone else later.

"You alright there love?" He asked, taking another step towards her.

Alice nodded. "I'm fine, Hatter. Lead the way, please."

He nodded, and with a bright smile, they continued walking.

The path felt like rubble beneath her flat shoes. She felt every stone, and whatever else lay on the path ahead. Eventually, they reached a crossroads. The two paths were separated by a larger tree, with a branch that stuck out ahead of them. A cat was perched on the end of it.

They were blue. No, they were purple. Actually, they were grey. They seemed to be a mix of all of these colours. Their eyes were sparkling like sapphires, almost too precious to be used on such a creature. They smiled at them as they stopped before them. Their teeth were white and sharp, and they stretched in a way they shouldn't be stretched.

Their eyes turned to Alice as their curvy tail lifted into the air. "Well if it isn't Alice, a *pleasure* to see you again." His voice was smooth, like the music with all the brass. They then shot a sideways glance at Hatter. "And *not* a pleasure to see you."

Hatter, though his eyes shone with a flare of anger, did not seem affected by the cat's comment. He tipped his hat and said with a charming smile. "The feeling's mutual Catto!"

The cat then focused their

attention back to Alice. "I haven't seen you in here in a while…how have you been?"

The cat then focused their attention back to Alice. "I haven't seen you in here in a while…how have you been?"

Alice folded her hands together and lowered her head, nodding once. "I have been well Mr. Cat."

They purred. It was loud and caused some of the leaves to fall off the tree. "Hmmm…how is the white room?"

She paused and took a second to think. She then answered. "White."

They huffed. "As it should be…have you gotten out of-,"

"Ali, I think we gotta get going," Hatter said suddenly, reaching for her hand. "We don't wanna be late for the tea party I've got set up."

"We were having a conversation." The cat said with a growl.

"It ain't an important one." He replied, his tone shifting to something serious that Alice had never seen in him. "Come on Ali."

Hatter started walking, whistling as he went. Alice noticed he looked back every second, slowing his walking down so that she could catch up to him.

She quickly looked back to the cat. "My apologies Mr. Cat, but I must be going."

They gave her a small smile, not nearly as stretched as the one they were originally greeted with. "It was lovely to see you again Alice, please do come back for a chat."

"I will thank you." She bowed her head and went to turn to the path Hatter had continued to walk down.

However, just as she was about to look over there, she noticed something out of the corner of her eye.

The cat noticed it too, and their gemstone eyes focused on it.

For you see, that's when Alice, for the first time, spotted the rabbit.

Follow That Rabbit

The rabbit was white. Like the room of white. It was the same shade, colour and identity as that room. Alice watched it with wondering eyes, as it ran past, springing across the forest path and scrambling down in the opposite direction Hatter was walking and whistling down. The cat perked up at the sight, and the rabbit stopped running for a second and turned to the tree, and Alice. It twitched an ear, tilted its head, and continued sprinting.

The cat shrugged. "Methinks the rabbit wants you to follow him."

Alice, still slightly stunned, looked to meet the cat's eyes. "Who's me?"

"That is an *excellent* question." The cat smiled. "Go follow the rabbit."

Alice jumped, flinching at the very sudden command. She scurried after the rabbit like she was the rabbit herself.

Hatter hadn't noticed she had gone.

She wandered down the other path, catching glimpses of white as she went further into the forest. Alice felt a somewhat wave of calm settle over her like a blanket. A sense of purpose was good. A direction to follow, a goal in sight was motivational. She remembered hearing that somewhere. Perhaps it was the courtroom. However, she did not know whether a card or animal had said those words, either to her or to someone else.

Regardless of words and what was said, not said or should have been said, Alice followed the rabbit. Further and further into the forest, she went. The tree turned less blue and more, well, tree coloured. They were dark, still dark. Always, always dark. However, in the opposite way to what she would expect, the forest got much brighter. Natural sunlight started to split and filter through the tree branches, bending and beaming down onto the forest floor. Small rays dotted the path, illuminating it. It was like Alice was following a trail of will-o-wisps.

The path seemed to open up in the distance, and Alice hurried towards it. She still saw the rabbit, it wove in and out of the trees, and now and then

Alice saw its big black eyes turning to look back at her. Almost as if it was making sure she was following.

She reached the opening in the forest. The stone path stopped, and her shoes sunk into bright green grass. She looked down, confused, and suddenly aware the entire time she had not bothered to properly absorb her surroundings.

So, in a spark of mundane logic, Alice looked up.

The clearing in the forest was encircled by trees, and there seemed to be no other paths. Flowers were growing along the trunk edges, all of them brilliant colours, colours that only the mind could conjure. In the middle of this grassy clearing were a round white table and two chairs. The table had a delicate-looking tea set arranged neatly on it. In one of the chairs, there sat a person that Alice had never seen in Wonderland before.

He wore black armour, that didn't seem heavy on him. He looked quite comfortable in it as if it suited him naturally. He wore no helmet, and Alice saw the curly brown hair that rolled down to his chin.

When he turned to look at her with his jade-green eyes, she instantly looked at the scar that ran down his right eye. The opposite side of where the scar on Alice's cheek was.

He looked too simple to be here. He was too out of place. Alice couldn't make sense of it.

"Oh hello," His voice was light like the wind, and his smile looked real and refreshing. "Would you like some tea?"

He gestured to the other seat on the table. Alice shook her head. "No thank you, sir. I'm sorry, I…I didn't mean to disturb you. I…I was following-,"

"A rabbit, yes I know." He nodded. "He wanted you to come, so he led you here."

Alice frowned, completely puzzled. "W…why…"

"That I don't know the answer to. You know this place better than anyone." He looked at Alice with worry. "Come now, don't look so frightened, there's nothing to fear. This is the safest part of the forest. Please, sit down." The black knight gestured to the chair again. His eyes were wide and welcoming, and Alice felt an odd sense of comfort.

"I…I should get back to my friend Hatter. Please forgive me, sir."

He frowned. "I…I would like to have tea with someone. I promise, once we've had a cup, I'll lead you back to your friend. You have my word." He bowed his head.

Alice looked back at where she had come from, and then back at the young man sitting at the table. His whole face was sad.

"The teapot's getting cold. I've been waiting here a long time."

She felt her chest tighten. Letting out a shaky breath, she looked at him firmly. "One drink…sir?"

"That's what I promised."

Alice nodded. "One drink."

His face turned into a welcoming beam, and he clapped his hands together twice, and only twice. Alice took a brave step towards the table, and the black knight quickly poured tea into one of the cups.

"Do you take sugar, dear?" He asked eagerly.

Alice sat down, her back stiff and rigid against the white chair. She felt slightly restless like something unexpected was going to happen. She looked over to the black knight and frowned. "I don't remember, sir." She said, finally answering his question. "I don't remember the last time I had tea."

He looked at her for a moment, his eyes squinting and putting a hand to his chin. He nodded once. "You have sugar."

He grabbed the sugar pot and a golden teaspoon. He carefully dropped one sparkling white sugar cube into Alice's cup and placed it back on the saucer. He pushed it towards her with a smile. "One drink, as promised. Just for you."

Alice lifted the cup and took a sip. Her lip curled. "It doesn't taste of anything."

The black knight chuckled. "It wouldn't dear." He shook his head. "It wouldn't."

She looked down at the tea, then up at the black knight. "I don't understand, sir."

He took a moment too long to reply. When he did reply, he didn't respond to Alice's questions or answers. "You may call me the Knave. What may I call you?"

"Alice, sir. Did you steal the tarts?"

The Knave paused and then burst into hideously joyful laughter. Alice felt her hands tremble, a sudden recollection rippling through her mind like a deep ocean wave. She didn't register the idea she had dropped the teacup until she heard it chip off the saucer and crack.

Alice struggled to hold back a cry, and her hands covered her ears as her wide eyes watched the tea spread across the white table like a puddle, dripping

off the sides. The Knave looked surprised but then noticed Alice's expression. "Oh dear, it's alright! It can be cleaned up!"
He quickly stood up and went over to her, kneeling on one knee in front of her chair. "Deep breaths Alice." He held up his hands, moving slowly towards her face. "Lower your hands. It's alright."

His hands reached hers, and she stiffened instantly. His hands felt warm, and she should feel comfort in them, but she didn't. The touch was all she registered because her mind always associated touch with the darkness that came with the person who touched her. He pried her fingers off from her mouth and lowered them into her lap.

"It's just tea." He said with a kind smile.

Alice didn't breathe for a second.

And another second.

And another.

It took her a long time to breathe. When she finally did, a familiar voice and a familiar figure appeared at the end of the path where Alice had entered the clearing.

"Ali! I finally found ya!"

Alice jumped at the voice. "Hatter!" Her voice sounded desperate and completely devoid of air. "I-,"

Hatter strode forward, and his steps skidded to a startling halt when he saw the Knave. He bent towards them both, a scowl beginning to form on his charming face. "What ya doin' to Ali?"

His voice became very sinister, and Alice recognised it well. The Knave stood up fast, and Alice got up and walked towards Hatter. "Hatter I'm sorry I-,"

The Knave took a step forward towards Hatter, holding up his hands. "I can explain. I invited her for tea and-,"

"The only one she has tea with is *me*."

The Knave looked extremely offended. "It was one cup-,"

"One cup too many." Hatter reached out and grabbed Alice's hand, pulling her towards him. She lost her footing and stumbled over the grass. The Knave caught her and helped her to stand straight. Hatter glared with a death-like stare at the both of them. "C'mon Ali, I doe trust him or these woods."

Hatter was gripping her hand awfully tightly. It was hurting Alice, and she felt her hand numbing to his touch.

"Hatter you're hurting me-,"

He tugged at her again, but the Knave didn't release her from his hold.

"This isn't helping!"

Words have power. Alice read that somewhere, once, a long time ago. She remembered where those words had been said before.

Before.

That was a long time ago.

Before she was not who she was. When she was someone else.

Alice saw nothing but black.

When Alice found herself in wonderland for the first time, Hatter was one of the first people she met. now at this time alice wasn't aware of how big the problem was, or how white the rooms would become. Hatter came at the moment Alice needed him the most, the temporary distraction from the hurt she thought was temporary. yes there were tea parties and exploring, rambling discusions about things that could have been discussed over tea. because Hatter is part of Alice from before and Alice met Hatter they had close conversations over tea and havit is doing now is preventing Alice from understanding the reality she is in and havit is doing now is preventing Alice from understanding. during this time Alice was not aware of the implications of the firm understandments, Hatter trusts Hatter,we find ourselves at a change Alice met Hatter they will refuse to see that Hatter is of the firm understanding the implications of the catastrophes of her mind, and thus herself and Hatter became firm friends on all accounts. however we have now reached a point where venting what must be done. The other people in wonderland are as aware of this as Alice. + she had, which now must change since we have reached this point. Hatter does not s will find ourselves in a much worse position.. their friendship is no longer a positive c ing in wonderland is linked. it is everything of alice and everything alice should and the time for that to stop. we have to help her before its too late Hatter needs to s ndher mindher mindher mi her mindher mindher m her mindher

Agreeable to Anything

"Ali? Ya there love?"

Alice opened her eyes carefully and slowly. Hatter was the only thing in her vision. She realised he was leaning down over her, his gemstone eyes glimmering. She gasped a little, and he smiled.

"There ya go! Come on now, get on up!"
Hatter took too gargantuan steps backwards, allowing Alice to stand up. She pulled herself up and looked around.

At her feet, was a yellow stoned path, though it was not actually made of stone, and only had the likeness of it. Instead of trees, flowers burst out from the ground. The colours were sickening to Alice, and the shape of the petals seemed almost unnatural. They bent and twisted, uncontrollable in their growth. Mushroom stalks strutted out of the dirt, twirling like corkscrews, and their round heads covered the ground like an eclipse. The sky was the same colour as it was before, and Alice could see more of it now.

They were out of the forest.

"What happened Hatter?" She slowly turned herself to look around. "How did we-,"

"Welp, that stupid bloody Knave made you collapse, so I scared 'im off. *Then* I carried you out of 'em woods, cause I never liked them anyway and-,"

"Hatter slow down please," Alice said in a quiet voice. A worry was wavering in her words. "The… the Knave didn't…I did not collapse because of the Knave, did I?"

Hatter nodded with a strong amount of confidence. "You did. He was sayin' all those things and it made ya fall over! I had to stop 'im from snatching ya away!" He put his hands on her shoulders. "He was gonna hurt ya Ali. We can't have that can we?"

"I suppose not." Alice nodded. "Forgive me, Hatter, I must not be thinking straight."

He tutted. "It's them dratted mushroom pieces. Poisonous, that's what they are."

"Hatter, I do not think-,"

Hatter had already started walking, for in his mind now that Alice was standing, it must have meant that everything was right again and there were no more questions to be asked. Alice followed him dutifully, and once again they were walking side by side.

"Are you gonna stay here Ali?" Hatter asked after they had walked in silence for some time. "I think ya should."

"I don't think I can Hatter. I believe they wouldn't let me."

He made a dismissive noise, like he did with every reason or excuse she gave to one of his ridiculous ideas. Alice did not like to think of them as ridiculous, but sometimes his thoughts got her into an awful lot of trouble.

"Look Ali, you core let people control ya like that. If it was me, I would just ignore 'em and stay here."

Alice shrugged, trying to be polite. "Well I am not you Hatter, and you are not me. Perhaps that is the reason why we sometimes disagree."

"Nah." He waved a hand at Alice. "It's cause you're stubborn."

She frowned. It was almost a scowl. Alice didn't have the capacity to properly scowl, so her attempt to make an angry face was her best.

Hatter laughed at this like he always did. Always attempting to make light of every situation the pair found themselves in. "Doe take it so seriously Ali. You've changed you 'ave. You used to laugh more."

Alice did not know how to properly react to this, for she could see some reasoning in his statement but at the same time, Hatter did not know everything, for Hatter blinded himself to many things.

"Perhaps you are right Hatter." She said simply, choosing her words with the utmost precaution.

"I'm always right." He replied triumphantly and continued joyfully walking through the mushroom-filled plains they had found themselves in.

They continued in silence, taking a turn towards some of the denser parts of the area. The mushrooms took more odd shapes, as if in some sort of rule-less competition to see who could take the most absurd form. They impacted against each other, their heads creasing and snapping against each other as they fought with one another in this endless game.

The two of them came across a split in the path.

Instead of two paths, there were several, and Hatter took a moment to finally assess where they had found themselves. As they paused in utter silence, there was a rustling behind the mushroom stalks.

Alice jumped at the noise, letting out a shivering whimper as her shoes scrapped against the stony path. Hatter turned to her, rolling his eyes with a chuckle, and resumed inspecting the uninspectable.

The rustling continued, and Alice held her breath, her eyes locked and focused on trying to locate the noise.

After only a scattering mix of seconds, moments and other small units of time, the source of the noise revealed itself. Its appearance caused Alice a make a frightened noise with her throat. The caterpillar was an odd shape, like most forms that we can conjure when we have very few restrictions on what is meant to be and what is not meant to be. It was like several not completely squashed circles were pushed against each other. Its head was misshapen, with a large chin and a forehead which was not as large. As for the colour, it was that odd mix of green and yellow, which to some would look sickly and to others would look dangerous. It had orange feet and hands if caterpillars have hands, or feet for that matter. Its eyes matched its hands, and it wore a silver monocle, in an attempt to look composed and formal. Even though he was a caterpillar.

Hatter immediately stood in front of Alice, holding out a hand and wearing a scowl that would frighten anyone *but* the caterpillar.

The caterpillar climbed over a low mushroom and sat. Pink cloudy smoke puffed out from his mouth. He peered at both Alice and Hatter with an unsatisfactory sneer.

"Who are you?" He asked.

Hatter's expression crossed a line between disbelief, confusion, and the misunderstanding of basic antagonism.

"You know who we are, we've been 'ere before!" He replied, his mouth snapping along with his voice.

The caterpillar let out a dismissive huff. "I know who you are. But who are *you*?"

Hatter paused, trying to define the absurdity of the sentence before him. "I'm Hatter." He replied eventually.

"Who is Hatter?" The caterpillar asked with a polite firmness.

"Hatter is *me*, obviously."

The caterpillar could see Hatter was getting more annoyed. His eyes spotted Alice behind him, and those eyes shifted to her. "Then who is she." He asked.

Hatter groaned. "She's Ali. Are ya gonna keep goin' on like this?"

Another puff of smoke, but this time it was purple. "Who is Ali?"

"She's her."

"Who is her?"

"Ali!" Hatter screamed, and Alice's heart jumped. His arms were flailing wildly towards Alice as if he was gesturing to some crazy absurdity.

"Who is Ali?" The caterpillar kept his strong neutral expression, which was something to be admired.

Hatter shouted babbling nonsense, finally cracking to the pressure of the straight-faced oddly shaped caterpillar. The caterpillar, seemingly satisfied that it had broken him, finally turned to Alice.

"Who are you?"

Alice bit her lip, assessing what her response should be. She decided to keep it simple. "I am me."

"Who's me?" The caterpillar's eyes had widened to something that looked akin to curiosity.

She thought about her answer. Then she remembered she had been asked this before. "That is an excellent question."

The caterpillar looked satisfied with her answer.

Hatter, however, was completely unsatisfied with the answer, and the entire conversation for that matter. He instantly grabbed Alice's hand and started gently tugging her away from the caterpillar.

"Come on Ali, let's go."

The caterpillar took a step in front of them with several of his many hands and feet. "Where are you going?"

Hatter looked at him with a smirk. "Away from *you*."

"I am not a place; I am a thing. What place are you going to?"

He sighed. "We're going to my house."

"Who's we?"

Hatter looked flabbergasted, which was a feat even for him. "Me and Ali. Are you dumb?"

"I'm simply asking. From my understanding, she never said she was with you. You two simply arrived here together."

"Well, it's obvious we're together then ain't it?"

"Not necessarily. Your paths could have crossed just at this sudden and precise moment. How am I to have guessed you two were heading to the same place?" The caterpillar huffed a little as he said this, with a puff of pink smoke pluming out of his round nostrils.

"We were walking up the path together, ya lump of idiocy."

The caterpillar looked marvellously offended, but he played it off surprisingly well. "I never saw that.

Just like I never saw nor heard her agree to come with you."

"Ya coulda assumed it? Ya saw us walking together!" Hatter's hands were turning to fists, and one of his eyebrows was twitching in irritating annoyance.

"Ah, and you see…" The caterpillar let out more pink smoke. "I don't make assumptions. It is never right to think you know everything or every situation. Each circumstance, person and idea is unique to itself, and we have no right to place judgement on any of them."

The caterpillar, in this particular moment, felt mighty proud to have bestowed his wisdom upon these two wanderers. Alice and Hatter's eyes met each other, in a moment of simply being stunned. Alice bore no outward reaction but found some logic in the caterpillar's words. Hatter, in the complete opposite sense, stomped his foot and scowled.

"That's a lotta nonsense and ya know it."

The caterpillar turned to Alice. "Did you agree to go with him?"

"I suppose I did sir," Alice said, still contemplating her surroundings and the intriguing ideas presented to her. "Hatter is my friend after all."

The caterpillar narrowed his eyes at Alice. "Just because he is your friend doesn't mean you instantly agree to everything he says. You seem to have a strong mind, so perhaps you need to start paying attention to the thoughts you have in there."

Alice was a little taken aback by the sudden but subtle attack, even if she didn't fully comprehend why the caterpillar was making such comments.

"Do you understand what I mean Alice?" The caterpillar asked, his words laced with infinite pressure.

Alice nodded. The caterpillar looked unsatisfied with her answer.

Hatter took Alice's hand once more. "Come on Ali, we've *seriously* gotta get goin'."

"I was never stopping you from leaving." The caterpillar commented.

Hatter's eyes seemed to burst with fire. "We know."

"Does she know as well or are you speaking on her behalf again?"

Hatter stamped his foot into the ground, sending pebbles scattering in all directions. He stepped forward and pointed his finger at the caterpillar. "Now you listen 'ere you gargantuan-,"

Alice gasped suddenly. "It's the rabbit!"

Sure enough, Alice's observation was correct. The white rabbit, the one she saw before, stopped in front of her. The same white as the room of white, a reflection of where she was before she came here.

She bent down to look closer, and the rabbit turned its head, moving towards one of the other paths. Hatter stopped his in-ranting tracks and looked at the rabbit. He groaned. "Not this rodent again."

The rabbit looked extremely offended. It jumped a little, then started going down the path, waiting for Alice to follow it.

"Ali come on; doe be so dumb," Hatter said, rolling his eyes.

"She's not being dumb. It's just a rabbit." The caterpillar added, causing him to get some unwarranted glares from Hatter.

Alice thought for a moment about what the caterpillar had said, and her unintentional way of following Hatter. She liked the rabbit. It was white, like the room of white, and that made her feel comforted somehow. It led her to that nice garden with the Knave. Perhaps, if her logic continued in this fashion, it would lead her to something similar.

She carefully walked behind the rabbit. She heard Hatter protest behind her, but she continued to walk. Her eyes were focused on the ground, and on the small rabbit that she was following.

Very suddenly, the rabbit stopped. Alice looked up. The Knave gave her a bright, truthful smile. "Hello, Alice. It's a pleasure to see you again."

A Walk Along Crossroads

"Now ya listen 'ere! I told ya to *leave Ali alone*!"

Hatter pushed against the Knave's chest. It was an unnecessarily violent, build-up of power that came forcefully pulsing out of one's hands in a furious moment of fiery pain.

The Knave, his body reacting perfectly to the brute force presented to him, stumbled back a little bit. He looked positively shocked at Hatter's reaction to his presence. "I was just taking a walk, Mr. Hatter. It is not my fault that we all crossed paths again."

His eyes glistened as he looked towards Alice. "She followed the rabbit, and he always leads you to where it wants you to go."

"I doe trust rabbits, and I doe trust *you*." He pointed a poked finger towards the Knave to actively back his bubbling words.

"Hatter please," Alice took a bold step forward, which was something memorable by her standards. "I had come across the rabbit before, and I was curious-,"

"Curiosity is what'll get ya hurt Ali!" Hatter spun towards her and gripped her arms. "All them times ya were curious, and ya used to sit there lettin' ya curious thoughts creep about and then ya-,"

"Stop talking."

Alice, through her flurrying mass of tears crowding around her eyelids, saw the Knave put his arm between them, and look at Hatter with a deep dark anger that she had never seen him conjure in the few instances she had met him.

"You just upset your *friend*. Perhaps you should apologise."

Hatter's mouth twisted, and his eyes flickered with rage. "I ain't listening to you."

"Regardless, the principle of the matter is you have upset your friend, and the right thing to do is apologise."

Hatter turned to Alice and cupped his soft hands around her thin pale face. His thumbs brushed under her eyelids, catching tears. "I was too 'arsh. But I was right, you know that, don't ya Ali?"

Alice, who knew exactly what Hatter was talking about, and remembered the consequences of her past actions, nodded affirmatively.

Hatter, still with his angry eyes, beamed and pulled Alice in for a hug. She gripped him tightly, feeling that rush of affection and trust. He had become the one true constant in her existence, and he would always be there.

As Hatter pulled away, the Knave offered a smile to Alice. His smiles never seemed to be directed to Hatter. "Why are you two wandering around here?"

"We're 'eadin to my house. You ain't invited."

"I guessed that." The Knave stated decidedly. He shrugged. "I actually know a shortcut. Would you both care to join me?"

"I doe wanna go anywhere with you." Hatter grabbed Alice's wrist and started pulling her away from the Knave.

Alice winced. "Hatter you're hurting me."

He let go. The Knave, watching with a righteous twinkle in his eye, spoke in a tone that many would consider ominous and foreshadowing. "There are many parts of this world where people can confront things, they're not ready to face. I will not stop you from going, but at least let me get you there unharmed."

"Look shiny boy, I know this place like the back of my 'and, I'll get her there in any way necessary."

Hatter turned to Alice. "Ya trust me don't ya Alice?"

Alice, who had been introduced to many a new possibility in her time here, was more than currently welcoming to the idea of following paths she had followed before.

"Of course, I trust you, Hatter."

The Knave looked betrayed, but he barely showed it. "Alright, I'm sure our paths will cross again Alice."

With an enormous reluctance, he turned and walked away. Hatter grinned. "Right then, let's get goin'!"

A Conversation Over Tea

Hatter's house was an amalgamation of many different atrocities and crudely designed architecture, but it was the house that Alice remembered fondly. It is often we find a fondness in things we find great comfort in, and this house, despite its questionable craftsmanship, still fell into this category.

The house was houses stacked on top of each other. Walls and sections of different materials, colours, and shapes were pushed together to seem like they had everything under control. The windows were the only consistent thing. They were square and white, but you could not see inside of them. Hatter was a very private person. The house started with a bright yellow front door with a golden handle and finished with a roof that stuck out its corners too far to look too reasonable.

Hatter kept his garden neat and ready for tea parties. There was a long table with an assorted of chairs and stools, for

Hatter seemed to be prepared for an infinite number of guests. The wooden table was laden with fragile tea sets, pots and cups and saucers with gold trims and delicate flowers were mixed. Cups were with saucers that didn't match. Each teaspoon was a different colour.

Taking her hand, Hatter guided Alice to one of the chairs. He picked a bright green one, with a pink seat cushion. He proudly stepped up *onto* the table and smiled at Alice from where she sat.

"As ya know, the only one who can have tea with you is me."

"It was only a cup, Hatter…" Alice replied quietly. "Was I wrong to try tea in a different environment?"

"You doe need different, cause nothin's wrong ya see." He started grabbing a red cup and a yellow teapot. "I doe know why ya had to go away…"

"I needed the mushrooms, Hatter."

"Pfft, ya doe know what ya want or what ya need Ali."

Alice shifted in her plush seat a little bit. "But… regardless of that, Hatter. Isn't it time for something to change?"

Hatter looked at Alice with a look that screamed *passionate defiance.* He assembled her cup of tea and poured the steaming liquid from the pot into her cup. He poured his own and sat down next to her.

"Look Ali, change means nothin' nowadays. Everyone up in that room is just telling ya to change. Change yer thoughts, change ya habits, change yer mind." He put a hand on her arm, the small comfort Alice needed at that moment. He smiled, wide and happy like Hatter always did. "It's all in yer head, there's nothin' wrong with ya."

She frowned a little. "I think that's the problem Hatter."

Alice took a sip of her tea. Even Hatter's tea didn't taste of anything. "Do I have this sweeter Hatter?"

He adamantly shook his head. "Nah Ali, that's how you've always had it."

She thought for a moment. "You must be right."

"I'm always right!" He put his legs up on the table. "Ya don't need Knaves or mushrooms. Ya just need me; I'm the best thing you've got."

Alice put her cup down, and it clinked back on the saucer. "I think the problem is me, Hatter."

Hatter rolled his eyes. "Nah, not this again. There's nothin' wrong with ya."

"What if there is? What if these moments I have are less than normal?"

"Everyone feels sad sometimes Ali, doe mean there's a problem."

"But they happen more often than not!" She clenched her hands and shuffled uncomfortably in her seat. "Surely I must be the problem."

"If this *problem* does exist, and I ain't saying it does, you would tell me about it."

"But sometimes I can't tell you about it."

"What's stopping you?"

"It's…" Alice struggled to state the obvious problem that was present and had been present during this entire conversation. But Alice was a cowardly person at heart, and that heart did not have the heart to admit her true feelings. "It's just that these problems can be overwhelming."

Hatter snorted a horrendous sound. "You're being ridiculous Ali."

"I'm not being ridiculous Hatter." Her bottom lip trembled while some deep sadness began to rumble inside of her. The rejection was often more troubling.

He smirked. "Well, that's all a matter of opinion. You say I'm being ridiculous, but *I* could say that you're being ridiculous." Alice could see his anger beginning to bubble over as his cheeks flushed scarlet. "I could say that the trees are ridiculous, or the sky is ridiculous, or I could say your hair is ridiculous. Actually, you know what I'm going to change my statement. I think your hair is ridiculous."

Alice, upon pure reflex, touched her dark brown hair. "That's not very kind, Hatter."

"Well *you're* not being kind, Ali. Talkin' down bout yourself and not once seeing that I'm tryin' to help you!"

"I merely suggested that I might have a problem-,"

Hatter cut her off with daggery words. "You doe have a problem, Ali! Ya makin' all this nonsense up!"

"But what if I'm not?" Alice stood up, never before feeling this mutilated in her entire existence of being alive.

Hatter slammed his hands on the table. "There's NOTHIN' wrong!"

Alice jumped at the sound of the slam, the sound rippling down into the depths of her mind. They were both standing up, staring at each other. Alice did not realise she was crying, but the tears were there, clear as crystal and gliding down her cheeks like her skin was nought but ice.

"Now look what ya done." He looked down at the table. "You made me spill my tea."

He reached for the teapot again. "I doe wanna keep doin' this Ali. Ya don't have a problem. There *ain't no problem*. Let's sit down and enjoy the tea."

As he poured the tea, keeping that small significant smile on his face, Alice realised that she didn't want to sit back down. For once, Hatter had made her truly angry. The constant reinforcement of the ludicrous denial would be enough to even Alice over the edge.

She turned and walked away, too wrapped up in pain to register the fact she had never wandered too far on her own before.

Hatter had always been her guide through this place.

But that did not matter now. Alice walked. She let her tea go cold.

take it easy

don't feel bad about it

i've caused a lot of pain

it alows I i didn't need them

Hatter won't like that please take them they will make you feel better please take them they will make you feel better please take them they will make you feel better please take them they will make you feel better please take them they will make you feel better

He never does, does he?

The king — as gave me the musk cms (×5)

The Road Those Lesser Have Travelled

Alice wandered back through the forest, on a path that she had never found herself alone on before. Hatter had always been a guiding comfort, a comfort that may have done more harm than good in the long run, but he had always been there. Now, however, Alice felt a smidge different than she did before. She could not concentrate clearly, her mind fogged and smudged by disillusions of dissociative damnations and emotions.

As she found herself walking, she noticed a familiar figure not too far ahead of her. It was the caterpillar. Still that odd shade of green and yellow, with its orange hands or orange feet. Alice still hadn't worked that part out. The caterpillar was in a grassy clearing not too far off the path, admiring the dark blue river that ran through the forest.

He must have heard her steps, as he turned his head towards her. "Oh. If it isn't you. Have you worked out who's me yet?"

"It still remains an excellent question."

"I wonder if one can ever answer such a thing." He moves his eyes back to the river. "Do you have a moment to stop and chat? We haven't had a proper talk in such a long time."

Alice realised she had nothing better to fill her mind or time with, so stepped off the path and onto the grass. It was dewed, and she heard it soften beneath her feet. She spotted a rock near the river, and she took a seat on it. It was a little cold, but Alice did not mind it.

She looked out over the river. She could see rocks peeking out over the top of the water, which meandered around their obstacles and kept flowing downstream. The sun and the sky were visible here since they were not surrounded by the forest trees and their harsh overgrowth. The sun made the water sparkle like it was filled with gemstones.

"Do you see the water, Alice?" The caterpillar asked.

"Yes, I do Mr Caterpillar." It's quite beautiful."

He nodded, satisfied again. "I have always liked how with the river water always finds a way around things. No matter what obstacle, with enough perseverance it pushes through."

Alice seemed to understand, and the caterpillar released a puff of pink smoke, with the wind pulling it in Alice's direction. She coughed. "You really should stop smoking, sir."

He huffed. "You really should learn not to follow that madman around."

"Madman?" Alice looked at him, stunned.

"You know exactly who I mean. He has not your interests at heart."

Alice was silent, and the caterpillar huffed out more pink smoke. "Smoking isn't good for you. It hurts your head."

He looked visibly annoyed. "I need smoke to clear my head."

"But the smoke makes your head worse."

"I need smoke to clear my head, but my head *always* hurts."

"That sounds like an awfully vicious cycle, Mr Caterpillar."

"It does, doesn't it? I want to clear my head, but there's so much smoke. It's hard to start seeing things differently when they've been the same for so long."

Alice looked back to the river. "Where do you get the smoke from, sir?"

He leaned his head further upstream. "There are flowers that grow by the riverbed."

"Perhaps it is time we get rid of them sir, so you stop smoking?"

"You really think it only takes one step, Miss Alice?"

"I think it is worth trying Mr Caterpillar. Change is hard, but it is possible."

He huffed once more, shifting on his orange hands or orange feet. "You don't seem to want to change when you're with Hatter."

"I…I'm not sure what you mean."

The caterpillar clicked his tongue. "Think for a moment, Alice. Hatter is very set in his ways, and you seem to follow suit. However, outside of his influence, you are a much more interesting young lady. That's why I wanted to know who *you* were, not what he deemed you to be."

Alice did not know how to respond. Truth was a fickle and harsh thing. So, the caterpillar continued. "Perhaps you're right. Smoking *is* bad."

Before she could react, the caterpillar shuffled upstream, his eyes trailing the riverbed. "Here we are." He announced. "Could you give me a hand, Alice? I have no hands."

They were orange feet.

Alice followed him and spotted, growing slyly on the riverbed, a cluster of pink flowers. Their petals were sharp and pointed, like knives, dropping over each other. A fine, darker pink powder settled on the stem and leaves.

"Are these what you smoke, sir?"

"Through no real choice of my own. Sometimes things happen suddenly, and you don't realise it's a problem until it's too late." His eyes slid over to meet Alice's. "How long did it take you to end up in the room of white?"

She thought for a moment. "Longer than it should have. I wasn't as aware as I should have been."

The caterpillar nodded. "Pick up those flowers and throw them into the river."

Alice bent down, knees sinking into the soft grass. "Are you sure about this sir?"

"Change is hard, but it is possible. Those were your exact words." He sighed, releasing one last, long puff of pink smoke. "Make sure you get to the roots."

Alice reached with both hands, grabbing all the flowers in her hands. She yanked, tumbling backwards slightly, as they lifted out of the ground. She managed to somehow regain her balance, and in her hands was a cluster of now decaying flowers.

The caterpillar looked down at her and sighed. "Do it."

Alice lifted her arm back and threw the flowers into the river. She stood up, dusting off her skirts and tights as she watched them drift downstream. The caterpillar looked despondent.

"I'm sorry, Mr Caterpillar."

"Apologies are not necessary Alice. It was for the best."

As Alice was about to respond with something of equal politeness, she gasped. "Sir…your back!"

The caterpillar turned so that he could see his body in the water's reflection. His eyes were also wide. Cracks had formed along his back, and from there, two pink crystal butterfly wings were growing.

"Hm. Interesting." Although his tone of voice with mutual, his expression was of magical awe.

"It only takes a step?"

"It seems that way, doesn't it?" The caterpillar shuffled again so he could face Alice. "So, when will you be out of that room of white?"

Alice shook her head. "No, sir, I...I think I'm beyond saving."

"Nonsense. Nothing is final. You'll be able to take that step eventually." He smiled at her confidently. "So, who are you?"

The answer was obvious even to Alice.

"I am me."

"Who is me, Alice? *Who is me?*"

This answer was not so obvious. She thought about herself, and who she was. That's when she realised, with or without Hatter, she had not been herself for a very long time.

"I think I have forgotten."

The caterpillar seemed satisfied with her answer.

A Different Path

"I must say my friend, I am simply adoring the new look!"

Alice recognised the voice, and she was amazed at who it was. When she turned her head, the Knave was standing on the same path Alice had been on. He had his hands behind his back, smiling happily as he tapped his foot.

"Hello again, Alice." He said warmly.

The caterpillar looked over as well. "I was waiting for you to turn up."

"I picked the right moment. I would have half expected you to be covered in smoke."

"I quit." The caterpillar looked at Alice a little as he spoke. "It was time to clear my head."

"I'm glad you did." The Knave replied, bowing his head. He looked at Alice. "I see you had some help?"

"She is a very interesting young lady."

Alice was stunned, and she felt her stomach plummet. Her hand reached for her mouth, and she looked away. "I-I'm not, sir. Not at all."

"Don't be ridiculous." The caterpillar rolled his eyes, fluttering his new wing attachments. "I think it's time for me to go."

She looked at the caterpillar. "What do you mean?"

"You can continue with the Knave. He'll take it from here."

Alice looked between the Knave and the caterpillar. They were sharing a look of mutual agreement. Alice was struggling to understand what they were agreeing on.

"It's been a pleasure, Alice. I hope you answer that question." He shuffled away, back over the mushrooms and into the thick of the trees.

The Knave offered Alice his arm, although there was still quite a distance between them. "Care to join me back on the path, Alice?"

Alice walked over but did not take his arm. The Knave looked disappointed. He had tried to hide it, but it was obvious. There were times when Alice just wanted to lock herself in, and this was one of those times. She hoped the Knave wasn't too upset with her, although he probably was.

"I'm sorry, sir."

He raised an eyebrow. "You have nothing to be sorry for."

He started walking, and Alice followed him. They carried on up the path, not going back the way they came. The forest was still the same. The trees hid away the sky, allowing skittering streaks of light to shine through only when it was convenient for them.

"I'm glad you were able to help the caterpillar."

She nods. "I hope he will stop having headaches now."

"Hm. I agree. Smoke tends to cloud judgement." He seemed to think for a moment. "May I ask you something, Alice?"

Alice's stomach tightened. "I-I suppose?"

"Do you think Hatter is a good friend to you?"

"I-,"

"Ali?"

She also recognised this voice, and she turned, slowly breaking into a shaky smile as she saw Hatter running up to her on the path. He greeted her with a hug, and he hugged her so tightly that she couldn't move her arms.

"Hatter…you're hurting me."

"Two more seconds!" He protested. He eventually let go, placing his hands on her shoulders. "Oh Ali, ya shouldn't have run off like that-,"

That's when Hatter noticed the Knave. "What are *you* doing here again?"

The Knave put his hands up defensively. "I was just walking with her."

"It's fine, Hatter. Be nice." Alice replied, her voice still shaking a little.

Hatter glared at the Knave once more, then looked back at Alice. "I'm so glad I found ya. I wanted to apologise for lashin' out."

Alice blinked. "Oh, it's quite alright Hatter. I-,"

"I know things 'av been stressful." He said, completely ignoring her.

She admitted she was a little stunned, and hurt, by this. "Thank you, Ha-,"

"*I* think it's cause it's been so long ya been down 'ere. Ya needed some time to calm down. Shouldn't 'av let ya tea go cold though."

Alice felt like she had been stabbed. Hatter had never been so dismissive before, at least not in her eyes. Her eyes drifted to the Knave, who was looking as disappointed as she was.

"Say Alice, would you mind if you walked with me? There's a lovely garden I've found."

"A garden?" Alice turned to him, excitement in her voice.

"Now hold on a minute!" Hatter stepped between Alice and the Knave. "Alice, we need to go back to my house. Ya don't need to be wanderin' around with strangers."

The Knave looked oddly smug. "Funny you say that. This garden is en route back to your house."

"No! No gardens, come on Ali." He grabbed Alice's hand, and he tried to turn them around and back the way he came, but she stopped him.

"I would like to see it, Hatter."

He froze. "What?"

"We can see it and then go back to your house. There won't be any harm to come from it."

Hatter looked at Alice and at the Knave. He was defeated by irreversible logic.

"Fine."

Wants and Needs

Alice found herself between two absolutes. The former was a warm gentle smile and a timid arm looped together. The latter was a scowl glued to a face and disgruntled steps next to her.

The Knave described their path in fascinatingly great detail. He spoke of the route and all the possible dangers that may befall on them on their travels to Hatter's house.

They were still in the woods. Everything Alice had seen thus far remained in the woods.

Hatter made it very clear the Knave was not permitted into his home.

Alice had become aware that she was in the company of two very different individuals. They became a very precarious balance that Alice had found herself in the middle of.

It had the means to topple.

The Knave had mentioned the garden contained a giant chessboard. Alice had always had a strange curiosity about the whos and whys of chess.

"What is this giant chessboard like Mr Knave?"

He looked utterly delighted that she had proposed the question to him. "Well, you see…hm…" He paused for a moment. "I have come to think of it like a garden of statues. Are you familiar with what I mean?"

She nodded. "It is similar to a garden of flowers, correct?"

"Yes exactly! But instead of flowers, it's a collection of statues."

Hatter cleared his throat. "Sounds borin' if you ask me. Statues are lifeless. No character."

"I could say the same thing about you."

Alice sighed inwardly, a silent sound that neither of them noticed. She always attempted to avoid conflicting conflicts or any sort of conflict for that matter. Her argumentative side was suppressive at most, almost non-existent. She took great joy in never having to use it.

Hatter chuckled. "Now see here Ali. Insults are no way to talk to someone. Never got anywhere by spoutin' insults."

"So, I cannot direct a carefully crafted insult aimed at a particularly loathsome individual. However, you insult my entire existence and ideals. You insult the person you have knighted your 'friend' and never give a natter about them as a person."

The Knave's counter was full of necessary comments. His tongue was taloned, or so it seemed to be.

Alice was left gaping, utterly unable to usefully use her argumentative side. This misdirective use of words had her confounded by speechless vowels.

Hatter, on the other hand, took the only rational solution he could think of in his questionable-sized mind.

He pushed Alice aside and his fist landed on the Knave's nose. She fell to the cobbled path, banging her head against one of the stones.

Her vision fuzzled, and all became a blur. Voices became muffled as there was shouting back and forth between the pair of characters. A defiant shout from the Knave seemed to bring Hatter into a temporary silence, and he bent down and helped Alice to her feet.

It took her a moment to regain her composure. When she looked again, the Knave seemed fine. Hatter's punch was wild and stupid, lacking coordination and timing.

The person in question had taken the opportunity to stand in front of the two of them, defensively putting his arms out.

"You're a reckless brat." Hatter proclaimed.

"I could say the same thing about you." The Knave replied.

That pre-mentioned argumentative side was starting to flicker back into existence.

At this point, Hatter burst.

"Get outta here! You 'av no right to be 'ere and no right to any words!"

"Hatter please…" Alice put a hand on her friend's hard shoulder, but he moved away and turned to her. Alice's ears were ringing. She was struggling to focus on her surroundings or the people with her.

"No, Ali! He's a bother! A disruptor! We are turning back and going *my* way!"

"Hatter…listen…"

"No! This ends now, no more wandering around, talking to people. We are goin' *back*."

He grabbed Alice's wrist, squeezing it in an angry grip. "Hatter…my head…"

"There's *nothin'* wrong."

Black spots were clouding her vision. With a little strength, Alice pulled on Hatter's arm and stopped him.

"Hatter-,"

"Why do ya trust him, Ali?"

"Because-,"

"He doesn't help ya with anythin', ya know that right?"

"I consider him a *friend*, like I do-,"

"He ain't no friend I'm your friend." He pulled on her arm again. "Come on."

Hatter seemed to be beyond reason at this point, and Alice felt his interruptions hitting her like a brick wall. Constantly smashing against her mind and confidence. Thus, with this action, she was placed in a situation where her argumentative side was warranted.

She took a breath again. "N-no Hatter."

He looked almost amused. "No?"

She nodded, regaining her balance. "The Knave described the route to me. Once we pass through the garden of statues, we are at your house. There is no point in turning back."

She looked at the Knave, who returned her expression with sad eyes. "We can part with the Knave then."

The Knave stood tall; hands folded with each other. He made no apology, but it was actively debatable whether one needed to be made.

Hatter stomped his foot. "Fine." He stormed past the Knave, heading back on the path. "Moron."

"I could say the same-,"

"Doe ya dare!"

This small victory made the Knave chuckle. He offered his arm to Alice, and with only a small hesitation, she took it.

Hatter never looked back.

"Your friend is quite mad."

Alice was completely frazzled, and it took her a while to form a response. "It's in his nature."

"His nature is to only fight for you when it helps him prove his point."

"He's my friend."

"And?"

"And…" Her thoughts stopped.

"You do not need to justify his actions."

"But I don't know what I need."

"Do you know what you want?"

Alice shook her head.

The Knave smiled. "Only you can work that out. Just know, as your *friend*, I know you have no need or want to defend Hatter."

"How do you know we are friends?"

He patted her arm as they walked.

"Because you needed one." He paused again. "Have you answered the caterpillar's question? He'll want an answer soon."

Alice thought, her mind racing as she comprehended everything that had happened. "I'm working on it."

The Knave looked satisfied with her answer.

They eventually caught up with Hatter. He looked mortifyingly discontented as he was standing in the middle of the path.

He pointed down into a clearing. "Look."

Alice looked.

Provoke the Beast

Hatter's pointed hand was directed towards a clearing in the woods. Bluebells were growing just off the path and grew down a hill towards where Hatter was pointing. The trees still surrounded them, and there was no sight of the sky yet. Alice had no means to look at it, and the sky had no means to look down at her.

The way towards this clearing invaded the tranquillity of the flowers. There was no clear path to walk down towards it.

"Come on, if we can take a shortcut, we can take a detour." Hatter rationalised, grabbing Alice's hand and leading her towards the group of trees that the bluebells led to. The Knave called after them, but Alice eventually heard his footsteps following.

Alice felt the flowers crushing beneath her feet. Blue among blue crumpled as her black shoes infected them.

They glided through into the clearing, where the trees had banded together to enclose an open space. To Alice's surprise and wonder, this space was not filled with bluebells. Daisies scattered themselves along the grass, peaking out over blades as if they were shy to every eye that would ever dare to look at them.

What was more surprising, however, was the beast that slept among these shy beauties.

Sealed eyelids closed sleepy eyes. Its snout was an empty tunnel, with two holes leading to its skull, and two thorn-like ears. It had no mouth since it did not need to speak words.

A spiney neck trailed down to its absurdly round body, which had sunk in places. Bat wings were lying flat over itself. The tail seemed to be made of blackened ribcages.

"Now ain't that a thing of beauty…" Hatter almost seemed breathless, his eyes glimmering and shimmering as they all stared at the beast. He turned his head to the Knave and sneered. "What do ya call that?" He asked in a cold whisper.

Alice whimpered. "It's the jabberwocky."

Beware the jabberwock. She had read that once. In a book long ago, back when things were kept imaginary.

"It shouldn't be here." The Knave said, stunned, and reached for Alice's hand. "Alice, let's go."

"Ha!" Hatter laughed, still keeping his voice low. "A jabberwocky! It's been *years* since we saw one of 'em."

He takes a step closer. "Last time was…well before them knights showed up and gave ya the mushrooms."

"Hatter, please be careful." Alice tried to add some assertiveness to her voice. "We don't want to wake it."

The assertiveness failed, and Hatter dramatically took another step towards it. Alice noticed how the beast breathed. It was deep and long, blowing away the petals that surrounded it. Almost like it was trying to push away the deep fear that consumed it.

Hatter reached for Alice, smiling. "Come on, might as well see what's changed bout it."

He dragged her through the daisies, and she ended up ripping many beneath her feet. She was pushed directly in front of it.

As she stared at the beast, eyes dead and breathing deadly, Alice saw the deep reflections of the distortions inside her mind. Somehow, the jabberwocky shared her blood.

"Hatter, I don't like this…"

"Alice!" She turned, and the Knave was looking at her begging, speaking harshly. "Come on, let's leave."

"Stop being such a coward!" Hatter chuckled. "It's harmless. See?"

Hatter kicked one of its feet. Alice's heart skipped, leaping through many impossibilities. The beast stirred, groaning slightly.

"Harmless." He kicked it again, this time around its stomach. Alice stumbled. A white door flashed in her mind.

The creature's eyes were moving.

Alice remembered the muffled voices of discontent. The start of the reckoning. The disappointment was rife all around her. People's faces became blank and expressionless, and she remembered not being able to form a solid connection with them. The loneliness she felt when the night came and she was alone, with only her destructive nature to comfort her. The fear was every day, it never stopped, never relented. She knew everyone expected better and was waiting for the day when she could be what she was before. But we as outsiders are well aware, that we are beyond that point. Outside this world, and in this one, she felt the agony the jabberwocky felt. It seemed even here she could not handle anything correctly. She was frozen still, as the same darkness of the jabberwocky started to consume her.

The Knave charged forward, just as Hatter stomped on its tail. "Hatter. Stop it."

Alice's hands went numb. Sharp stings shot through her hands and into her fingers. Her stomach became a void and her heart felt heavy.

The Knave forcefully pushed Hatter, and the creature let out a low growl. Alice felt it in her lungs.

"Alice, we need to go. Come on…"

The Knave stopped his words, and he turned. The jabberwocky's eyes opened.

Alice screamed.

Reality

Alice took a tumble.

        Down.

                Down.

                        D
                        O
                        W
                        N

                She went.

"

    We're lucky.

                "

Knives hurt.

    cut cheeks.

        cut hearts.

            cut minds.

"

        Why didn't she call us?

                "

Refused

Refused

Refused

        She said no.

Alice please stop crying.

Come on sweetie.

It was an accident.

See.

    You're fine.

        Just a cut.

See?

            D

            O

            W

            N

He's been around again, hasn't he?

                        DOWN

He always makes her do this.

                        We thought we
                        were getting
                        somewhere.

No time for that now. She needs to calm down.

Alice?

        Alice?
                    Down.

Alice.

We're going to give you something

                                          So you can go to sleep, okay?

Go to sleep Alice.

                                                Down.

She fell.

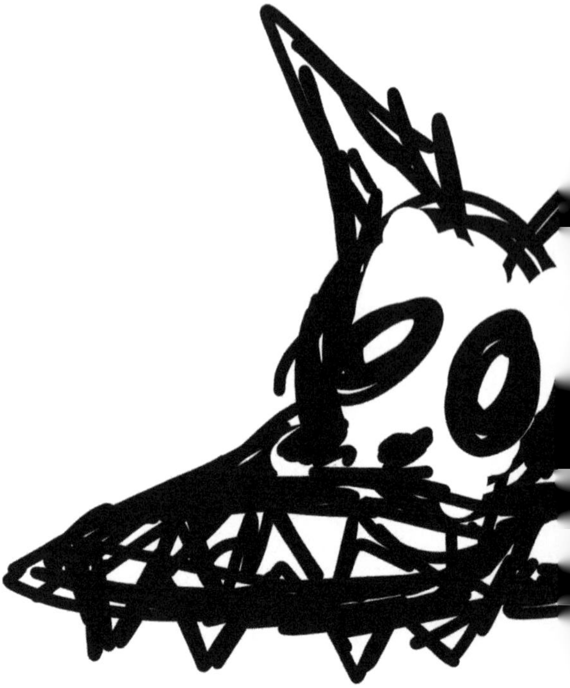

Time To Go Up, Alice

Alice woke up on a mushroom. She was back in the forest, back to where she first met Hatter again and back to where she first encountered the Knave.
As her dazeful eyes wandered up, she spotted the Cheshire cat once again, smiling down at her.

"You were expecting the room of white, weren't you?"

"That's where I usually wake up when I start screaming Mr. Cat."

They nodded. The cat leapt down from the twisted tree it had nestled itself in. "The Knave asked me to keep an eye on you."

"Why?"

"Because his eyes couldn't be here."

She looked around, and it suddenly hit her that someone was missing. "Where's Hatter?"

The cat shrugged. "He got into a horrible shouting match with the Knave after you disappeared. Stormed off in a mad way, as he does."

She nods slowly. "He does do that a lot."

"How incredibly perceptive your eyes are. If only your mind was the same."

She frowned. The cat continued to glare at her. "What happened after you disappeared?"

"I don't remember."

Down. Down. Down.

"All this disappearing and reappearing must stop. Eventually, you're not going to be able to place yourself properly."

"What is the need to place myself properly?"

"Everybody must have a place, Alice. It delays the mind from wandering aimlessly."

"It is nice for the mind to wander."

"Yes, but wander too far and then we find ourselves in awkward situations." They crossed their paws over each other. "Like this one."

"This is awkward?"

"Awkward for me. I would much rather *not* have to feast my eyes on the sad little girl who should be a woman."

Alice was about to open her mouth to determine her reply, but then she noticed the rabbit.

"Ah, the Knave's brave and bold messenger. Come to lead Alice away to her destiny again?"

The white rabbit, who probably felt incredibly infuriated, twitched one ear down to the right. Alice leaned forward and noticed the mushroom was positioned on the edge of a path. This was not a path that Alice recognised. It was the path that those with fragile minds travelled less, and those similar to Alice travelled lesser.

The rabbit continued to twitch his ear down the path.

"It seems our time is up Alice."

"I thought time always went down."

"It wounds down, it never goes anywhere."

"Everything has to end up somewhere Mr Cat."

"Precisely. And you need to end up following that rabbit. Like everyone in this kind of story does."

Alice slid off the mushroom, and her feet thumped on the path. She turned back to the cat in the tree, with its jewelled eyes and unforgiving smile.

"I wish you the best Alice. We will not be seeing each other again."

Alice was confused by this. Nobody here ever talked like that. So final and absolute. It had never occurred to her once that perhaps all decently good things must come to an end. She had read that somewhere, but only now had the words finally taken hold. The Cat had always been a tricky sort, but it always knew exactly how it must be, and Alice finally saw that.

"Thank you, Mr. Cat. I wish you the best also."

Alice blinked, and when she had finished, the cat was gone. It had only left behind the very *idea* that it had been there in the first place.

She looked to the rabbit, who was eagerly ready to show her down the path. She nodded and started to walk behind it.

Alice took this moment to fully take in what was surrounding her. This part of the forest seemed brighter somehow. The trees did not look so sickly, and it reminded her very distinctly of spring. The leaves were bright and green, slowly developing into a brand-new life that it had planned out for itself. Sunlight blasted through the branches, golden yellow and illuminating her skin in brief intervals.

Alice found herself thinking this part of the forest was truly beautiful.

"What a curious path I have found myself on."

The rabbit squeaked in agreement.

A Conversation Over Tea

Eventually, they found themselves at the chosen destination. It was another clearing, and at this point, it was obvious Alice constantly found herself in clearings like they were openings to new truths and ideas.

Paths had to lead somewhere, she supposed. The rabbit guided her in, but as soon as she turned around, it was gone. To put it simply, it had led her onto her final path, and now it didn't need to guide her any more.

However, Alice saw the Knave in the clearing. The scene was an instant replica of their first meeting. The setup was exactly alike. The clearing was edged with flowers, the table and chairs. And the Knave, in his armour, holding a teacup in his hand, removing a part of a carefully arranged tea set.

He smiled at her. "Does this feel familiar Alice?"

"I believe the phrase I should use is déjà vu?"

He chuckled, causing Alice to flinch again. He stood up and walked over to her. "You do know it's time for you to go, right?"

"Go where?"

"Go home."

Alice was startled. "Home?"

The Knave looked saddened by the events. "You can't stay here anymore Alice. It's not safe, not for your mind."

"My mind needs some mushrooms."

"Exactly. And your mind won't get them here." At that moment, he offered his hand. "But before you do, we are finally going to have some tea."

She took his hand without hesitation. He carefully took her to the table and sat her down. "Didn't we have tea before?" She asked.

He shrugged, as he started preparing everything. "You took a sip before we were interrupted. I'm going to at least let you have a cup."

She looked around. "Hatter's tea parties were a lot more chaotic than this."

"Hatter *is* chaotic." The Knave replied with a grumble.

"I have been thinking…" She paused for a moment to think about what she truly wanted to say. "That perhaps Hatter wasn't the nicest friend."

The Knave put Alice's cup down, filled with tea. He spoke slowly, treading on fragile shells. "What makes you think that?"

"I…it might be me being mad but…he never seemed to care." She slowly went to pick up the cup. "He wanted me to stay here, but…I'm starting to believe it wasn't for the right reasons."

He sat back down with his cup. "You truly think that."

It took a second, but Alice did nod. "He said it was because it was best for me, but maybe it was best for him because he likes things a certain way…" She sipped her tea. "He was never a lover of change."

Alice tasted the tea and frowned. "It's not sweet enough."

The Knave looked surprised. "It isn't?"

She shook her head. "No…I just remembered I like it sweeter."

Before she could move, the Knave dropped another sugar cube in. Alice sipped it again and smiled. It was sweet enough.

He sipped his tea and then looked back at her.

"Have you changed?"

She paused. "Maybe I have. I have let Hatter control me for too long. Comfort isn't always a necessity. What I want and need are now two entirely separate matters."

"You are a very different Alice from the one I first met."

She gave him a light smile. "I like this Alice too…I think I do want to go home Mr. Knave. I no longer like this place, no matter how beautiful it is. There's something beyond the room of white."

Alice noticed the Knave had tears in his eyes. "Yes Alice, there definitely is." He put down his cup. "Are you finished?"

Alice had been drinking her tea throughout this conversation and looked down to notice her cup was empty. "I finished it this time."

"Excellent." He stood up. "Now, before you go, there is one last person who wants to meet you."

"Who?"

"You'll see soon enough." He offered an arm to her. "Come on, let me lead you this time, no rabbits, I promise."

She nodded and stood up, taking his arm. He guided her out of the clearing, and back onto the path.

Some time passed, and the Knave had taken Alice out of the forest, and that was when Alice saw where they were.

A great grey castle towered over the horizon.

Towers soared in every corner, with twisting spires and curved battlements. Banners were hung down the walls. Iron bars slid down the cuts in the stone that made the windows.

Alice felt a twist of fear in her stomach, but the Knave touched her arm gently as they approached the black gates. There was a guard on the other side, dressed in the same black armour as the Knave. This knight had a helmet on. It was black and streaked with silver. Beyond him, Alice could see the castle entrance, and the path leading to it. A long path lined with rose bushes. Red and blooming like a pool of blood.

"We're here to see the Queen. I have arranged a meeting between her and this young woman here, named Alice."

The guard had an intense level of understanding and opened the gates for them. They clattered shut behind them, and Alice walked side by side with the Knave, all the way up to the castle doors. Two guards in helmets opened them, and the unlikely pair stepped into the throne room.

So, how did you find Alice? So interesting to talk to. Is that why she's here? She's a unique girl, isn't she? If only she saw herself that way. You being there is enough. She's quite the lonely one. I want to help her somehow. Unfortunatley so.

Knaves and Queens and Other Logical Things

The first thing one could say when describing the throne room, was that it was tall. The windows at the end of the room stretched up to the skyward ceiling. They were made to look like roses surrounded by hearts.

In front of the windows was a set of grey stairs, leading up to a red throne. There was someone seated upon it, but from this distance, neither Alice nor any other eyes would be able to see who it was.

A ruby rug rolled down from the stairs towards them. Alice shuffled her feet and felt the static from the carpet. Guards were posted along the walls, straight and static in black armour. It almost seemed like they had no life in them at all. There was a chance you would not be able to hear them breathe.

The room was very red, both in its mood, emotion, and presence.

The Knave pushed them both forward, his steps as regimented as the guards. He stopped just before the stairs ascended. "Your Majesty," He called upwards. "I present Miss Alice."

The figure on the throne stood up and descended the stairs. It was at this moment Alice could see her much clearer than when they first entered the room. Her dress, like everything else, was red and black, but covered in sideward stripes. Her skirt flowed out, dragging down the stairs as she made her way to them. A silver crown was stuck on her head, nestled between black curls.

As the Queen approached them, Alice recognised the face. The darkened eyes, thin lips, pale skin. It was a face of royalty, and in some obscure way, it was Alice's face too.

Alice had read in many books that you bowed to queens or anybody else who shared that title, but the Knave didn't move and merely kept eye contact with the supposed ruler.

The Queen regarded Alice for a long moment, lifting a hand to touch Alice's scarred cheek. Her touch was cold, and Alice did not like feeling. It felt like icy ruin.

"Pleasure to finally meet you, Miss Alice," The Queen dropped her hand with sheer elegance. "You have been wandering around for quite some time, and yet our paths have never crossed."

"Were our paths meant to cross your Majesty?"

"Don't call me that." The Queen shook her head, and Alice felt her hands intensify with intense stiffness. "Titles are formalities and formalities are fickle at best. You should never have to look up at somebody and see them as above you."

"Why?"

"Because in this mad world, we should consider ourselves equal."

For lack of a more descriptive word, Alice felt afraid. The air was heavy, and something was brewing, around her. Ideas, thoughts, and self-assessments were shifting out of their normal boundaries.

"Now," The Queen presented no time for such contemplative thoughts. "Would you care to take a walk with me, Alice?"

Alice looked to the Knave, to see if she could find guidance in those guiding eyes, and he smiled at her. "It's alright Alice; a walk would be good for the both of you. Her Majesty can take you to the garden that I was going to take you to."

The Queen offered Alice her arm. "Let us walk together, if only for a short while. I know you do not have long left."

With some slight reluctance, Alice took the Queen's arm, and the Knave gave them both a confident smile and watched them walk. As they stepped out of the throne room, the doors shut behind them.

The hallway in which they walked down towards this mystical garden; the Queen's eyes glanced to Alice. "You have something to say. Or even better, something to ask."

It was true, though Alice did not dare to admit it, that for once she found herself asking the curious questions.

"Why does the Knave have to call you your Majesty and I don't?"

The Queen rolled her eyes and replied with a light smile. "Because I need to have *some* level of authority over what goes on here."

Alice's reaction was not usual for her. She smiled back at the Queen, chuckling slightly at the comment. She found some absurdity to the answer, believing there was some practical reason for the social custom and exchange. In actuality, the Queen just needed to assert some control over her rogue Knave.

"I think I just found some light in that tragically dark mind of yours." The Queen triumphantly said. "Now come, the garden is just ahead."

Go Away From Here

The garden fully shattered all expectations Alice had initially thought in her mind. Gardens, from Alice's own small and imaginary experiences, were lacklustre and plain. The simplest of flowers were arranged in the simplest of ways to conform to the simplest ideas of beauty the world around her seemed to have.

This garden, however, had thrown out the very idea of simplest and had declared it wordless.

The statues were exactly as the Knave had described them. They were chess pieces, made of shiny black and white stone. Mayhaps it was marble, mayhaps it was stone, but Alice was not one to decipher such things. Red roses grew around them, purely a symbol of the Queen if one was to analyse it.

Along the path they walked on, daisies grew between the cracks. With every step, more of them grew, never being held back by the hard material they constantly encountered.

Alice looked up and breathed in the sky. She had been bustling and bumbling through woods and trees and had very rarely accounted for the sky above her. The infinite blue space that kept this world encompassed in its invisible hands. It was clear and calm at this moment, reflecting on how Alice felt about herself.

Some would say that Alice had been on some kind of journey. Others would suggest that Alice's journey was purely imaginary. Alice would say she fell down.

The Queen was holding Alice's arm, and she stopped walking as Alice observed the sky with darkened eyes.

"I wonder what's up there." The Queen mused.

Alice looked down and met the eyes of the red ruler. "What do you mean?" She replied, remembering the rules about titles and authority.

"Well, you fell down didn't you Alice? If you came down, it makes one wonder what you came down *from.*"

"There's nothing but white rooms up there," Alice said with a shudder.

The Queen shook her head, dismayed. "There is more up there than white rooms. Surely you know that Alice."

Alice covered her mouth with her free hand, shaking her head as if to rattle some complex insecurities. The Queen moved Alice's hand away. "Now we'll have none of that. Let's continue walking."

So, they did. Alice wondered why the Knave was so eager for Alice to see this. Of course, it was a stunning piece of architectural and agricultural brilliance. Alice didn't think those were the right words in the right context, but alas there were more pressing matters to handle.

"Do you know why I had the Knave bring you here?"

What an awfully conveniently timed question and thought that turned out to be.

Alice shook her head, and the Queen, curled a piece of hair behind her ear, adjusting her crown with one hand. "It is because you are not yourself, Alice. You have not been for a long time, and to be quite frank it has passed the point of ridiculous."

When the Queen looked to Alice for a response, all she got was a blank expression. Alice did not know how to respond because admitting such a truth was always the hardest part.

The Queen muttered something harshly beneath her breath, making Alice's heart thud with trembling fear. "This place bears the weight of being with you Alice, and as such I am part of it. You should not be who you are now."

Alice was left with a thousand trifling questions. Common sense was no longer rational, but whether it was in the first place is up for discussion. Words such as these had not been dared said in such a long time.

"Then who should I be?" Alice asked.

"Anyone but this."

They stopped walking. At this point, they had reached the centre of the garden. The rose bushes surrounded the path in a circle. There was a pond in the middle, with shining, pearl-clear water. The Queen put both her hands on Alice's shoulders, which in turn made Alice feel very tense.

"It's time for you to go now."

Alice did not even need to ask what the Queen meant. This whole conversation about being and going and what is up, all seemed to connect.

"But…I don't want to leave."

"If you don't go now, you never will." The Queen put a hand to Alice's face again, pushing some of her hair away from her eyes. "It's time to say goodbye, Alice."

That fear was sitting in Alice's chest because she knew the Queen was right.

"It won't work unless you say it yourself." The Queen hinted with a whimsical smile.

Alice nodded. "It's time-,"

"Ali?"

Suddenly, in that moment, everything came tumbling down again. A reminder of what had emerged in the garden. Hatter came bumbling down the path. His hat was still lopsided, his clothes a mess of over-enthusiastic ideas. His smile was the same, still jolly and carefree.

"Ali there ya are!" He burst forward and trapped her in a tight hug, pushing the Queen aside.

"Hatter, what are you doing here?" Alice asked, trying to push herself out of his arms.

"Yes, what are *you* doing here?" The Queen added.

Hatter let go of Alice, keeping one hand on her shoulder while turning to the Queen. "I'm 'ere to see Ali, we're *friends* ya see."

The Queen picked herself up off the ground, dusting off her royal dress. Her face was locked in disgust. "And last time I checked you were not welcome here. This is my castle and my garden, only I say who can come and go."

"I climbed over the wall. Ya should keep an eye on those things." He retorted with a sly chuckle. "Now come on Ali, let's get out of here."

He took her hand and tried to pull her away again. He always did, leading her down impossible paths and taking her into parts of this land that probably shouldn't exist.

But Alice stood her ground.

"No Hatter."

He stopped. "What?"

"The Queen is right. You're not allowed to be here. You need to go."

"I am going." He tugged at her hand. "But I want ya to come with me."

Alice took a shaky breath. "I'm leaving Hatter."

"Yes, you're leaving 'ere. *With me.*"

"No, I'm leaving here." Her eyes wandered upwards. "I'm going back. It's time for me to go."

Hatter blinked at her; his mouth twisted into a snarling frown. "Back to what?! A room o'white and nothin' more?"

"There's something beyond that room, and I'm going to start seeing what it is." She felt her eyes filling with tears. "Please don't be mad."

"Mad…" He laughed, so much so that Alice shook. "Mad? Ali, I'm FURIOUS. After all this time, after everythin' I've done to help ya, you're just gonna leave?"

"I'm going Hatter, and you can't stop me."

"Ya makin' a mistake Ali, listen I need you to-"

For the first time, Alice interrupted him. "No Hatter I need YOU to-"

go away hatter i need you to go away now can't you see it's time it's time it's time no more of this we both know this isn't good or right for anyone my mind is a mess and i am no longer in control go away go away go away hatter there is more to life than white white is cold and thin and pale and everytime white is around i fall can't you see i fall i fall down down down maybe there are more books to read and chess to play people to meet and ask about their life and their ideas and their knowing i wonder who they are and if they have a story too hatter it's time for me to go i have to go away and you need to let in i have to go and you need to go too wonderland is no longer mine or yours or ours it's become something we can't control we made it to attempt to hide i did for years forgetting trying to forget forget forget forget what a mess i had become please hatter i need you to go you are the past i do not wish to remember please please please please let me move forward now and let you go go away hatter go away i need you to go away your voice can't plague me anymore i need to get better i need mushroom pieces and libraries i want to smell the wrinkled pages and touch the spines and feel the love pouring in every single page i want to smell the flowers and walk the garden paths and feel alive again this has been my refuge for so long that now it is beyond ridiculous i want to get out of the room and see what more there is maybe there is a wonderland of my own let me welcome it i need you to go away hatter go away hatter i don't want to see you anymore go away hatter go

GO AWAY HATTER

Alice fell up.

Are You Ready?

Alice was in the room of white. She was sitting on a white bed, with its white sheet and white pillow. Her knees were trembling. She interlaced the thin pale fingers on her thin pale hands and rested them in her lap.

But it wasn't completely white, this room. Yes, the walls were white, and so was the floor and the ceiling and the door, but there was a small window, with white bars over it. Some part of the outside could be seen if Alice opened the curtains.

There was a bookshelf, bare and needing more spines to fill it. There were a few stories stacked on there, but not enough. An eclectic mix of chess pieces was gathering dust. The wardrobe door was shut, with barely any of its outfits worn. This room needed some love and attention, as did the person inside of it.

There was a knock at the door, which brought Alice back to the present moment that she had found herself in. The door opened, and for what seemed like the first time Alice noticed the cream walls beyond the door.

"Morning Alice!"

Alice suddenly remembered who this person was. Doctor Oakwood had curly brown hair that he always tried to tie back. His face was old but welcoming and his eyes beamed nostalgia. He wore a green jumper and a pair of brown trousers, with a white shirt underneath. His shoes matched, and his monocle hung from around his collar. Alice had only just begun to notice the colours.

"I'm doing well, thank you, sir."

"Now Alice," He stepped inside. "We talked about this. There's no need for such formalities."

She noticed what was in Dr Oakwood's hands. He had a glass of water and a small clear container. "I want no fuss, alright?" His tone had suddenly changed to something very serious. "You need to take them."

He handed Alice the glass and opened the container, revealing two red mushroom pieces inside. Alice remembered what she had said goodbye to, and who. She knew this was for the best.

She took the pieces, and with a sip from the glass, she swallowed them.

"Well done Alice, I'm proud of you." Dr Oakwood went to open the curtains, letting the yellow beams streak in. Alice could see the dust in the air. "Right, do you remember what today is?"

Alice shook her head, so he continued to speak. "Today is the day you're going to leave this room."

Alice was stunned, and as she looked around, her hands shaking just a little bit, he smiled at her.

"Remember? You've been making such good progress, and since we have some extra hands today, we're going to get you out of here for a little bit."

"I…I think it slipped my mind…" She said, ashamed.

"Not to worry, we can walk down there, why don't you get yourself dressed?"

With a nod and reassuring thumbs up, Dr Oakwood left, shutting the door behind him. Alice pushed herself up off the bed and went to the wardrobe. She found herself not recognising any of these clothes, as she had not worn them in such a long time. Eventually, she settled on some black trousers and a white shirt with a flowery pattern she had forgotten she had and liked.

Alice brushed her hair and looked into a mirror. She hadn't seen her face in a long time. She had forgotten the shade of brown her hair was, or how the scar on her cheek had hardened the skin on her face.

It seemed that Alice was finding herself again.

Dr Oakwood, as promised, was waiting outside for her. They started walking down the cream hallways, and Alice looked out of all the windows as they did so, seeing all the colours she had only ever seen in her mind. The world was often dull when you had a dark perception of it.

"So Alice, how have you been feeling? Do you think things have been getting better?"

There was a brief moment of silence. For Alice, none of this felt real. There never really was an ending in sight.

"Dr Oakwood, I think I've gone quite mad."

He looked at Alice, his face in constant thought. "Yes Alice, you're mad. But we all are, in some way."

Alice looked stunned. "You stole that from a book."

"No, my dear, I stole that from *you*."

They turned a corner and went into a large room. Round tables with comfortable-looking blue chairs filled the floor. The walls were also blue, but it was a lighter shade. There were already people in the room, faces Alice didn't recognise. They blurred as she tried to recollect the names they owned. Games were scattered on the tables, already being played and absorbed by everyone.

He led her to a small table at the back, where somebody was sitting. As this person looked up, Alice's heart stopped.

It was the Knave.

But it wasn't, all at the same time. He looked exactly like the Knave who she had followed rabbits to. Who knew what tea she liked and how sweet she liked it. He who walked with her to castles and to meet queens.

"Alice, you remember Peter, right? He's one of our volunteers, always made sure to check up on you."

Peter waved. "Hey Alice, it's good to see you."

Alice smiled a little. "Hello."

Peter was wearing a white shirt and blue jacket, with blue jeans and red shoes. She was so used to seeing that face with black armour, that it was a little strange.

Dr Oakwood nodded to Peter. "I leave her in your capable hands."

He walked away, and Peter gestured for Alice to sit down. "I'm thinking we could play some chess. I bet it's been a while since you've played."

Alice sat down, her back straight. She looked up at him. "Yes…it has. I hope I've not forgotten how to play."

"I'm sure it'll all come back once we get started… oh! Before I forget," Peter bent down and picked something up by his feet. "I got you a gift."

"A gift?" Alice asked curiously.

Peter's cheeks went slightly pink. "I know you had that slip up a few weeks ago, but Dr Oakwood has been saying how well you've been doing so…"

He handed Alice a stuffed rabbit.

Admittedly, Alice was slightly jarred at first. But then as she looked closer, she realised it was a white rabbit, all too similar to the one she followed back in her wonderland. It had those same sweet eyes, and ears that could be flopped, to allow it to truly express itself.

"I know you like rabbits. And…" He handed Alice a book and quickly went about setting up their game.

She looked at the cover and realised it was her favourite story. Of a little girl who fell down a rabbit hole, and into a world which was beyond any reasonable reality.

Alice had not read this story in a long time, but she remembered every word of it.

As she opened the cover, she saw what was written on the first blank page.

Let this book be your wonderland.

Alice could have contemplated for a moment what that truly meant. What any of this meant. Or she could find herself purely and wholly content with the fact that her reality was found, and her wonderland was to be kept safely to the constraints of words and pages. But as we all know, some things don't go away so easily. There would always be something to set it off, to bring us back to the brink of madness. Ridiculous thoughts could not be ridiculed by one's self without some proper preparation beforehand, and Alice needed to learn to fortify her defences.

But for now, at least, she was content.

As she thought about this, she looked down. She saw the blue floor turn to black, and it started to cave in on itself. The fear was rising in the air, and she couldn't hear herself breathe.

"Alice?"

She looked up. Peter was smiling, holding a white pawn in his hand.

"Are you ready to play?"

Alice looked back down at the floor.

Everything was as it should be.

She smiled at Peter, the truest smile she could conjure.

"Yes, I'm ready."

Alice picked up the black pawn.

Acknowledgements

This book wouldn't have been possible without the love and support of so many people.

To my parents, thank you for putting up with me while I was a literal beast to deal with. Thank you for taking my problems seriously and not giving up on me.

To my little brother Sam, thank you for constantly interrupting me while I was writing, even though it was unintentional. Love you.

To the rest of my family, for being super nice and all that jazz. I bet I'm still not the cool member of the family now.

To my friend Hina, your endless enthusiasm shows no limits, thanks for constantly bombarding me with love when I didn't believe I deserved it.

To the entire party (past and present) of The Killing Game, thank you for loving Alice, for protecting her innocence, and crying for her when she died. Thank you for inspiring the characters in this book.

To Dorian, once again, thank you for being the most wonderful friend ever.

And to you, dear reader, thank you. You didn't have to take a chance on this book, but you did. And I appreciate that so much. Thanks for making my dreams come true.

About the Author

Emma (she/they) is an author, artist, jack of all trades and being of chaos. She is an absolute nerd (and proud of it).

Her published works are all independently produced. Yes, this means they are very tired.

When they're not writing, Emma is either in the theatre (both onstage and backstage) or rolling a d20.

She can be found on Instagram, TikTok, Twitch Twitter and YouTube if you search "PixieStarr"

They are aware that they are talking in the third person, and will stop doing so now.

Milton Keynes UK
Ingram Content Group UK Ltd.
UKHW020633101123
432322UK00018B/807